24
—
7

24 x7

A DECADE OF 24-HOUR COMICS

by ALec LONGSTRETH

PHASE
SEVEN
COMICS

PHOTO PANELS FROM "THE PAM ARTIST" WERE COPIED
FROM THE FOLLOWING SOURCE MATERIALS:
- NAKED CITY BY ARTHUR "WEEGEE" FELLIG
- BYSTANDER: A HISTORY OF STREET PHOTOGRAPHY
  BY JOEL MEYEROWITZ & COLIN WESTERBECK
- AMERICAN CENTURY: 100 YEARS OF CHANGING
  LIFESTYLES IN AMERICA BY RALPH ANDRIST

ISBN: 978-0-9853004-6-3

TABLE OF CONTENTS

Welcome to 24x7
A DECADE OF 24-HOUR COMICS

by ALEC LONGSTRETH

HEY! THAT'S **ME**!

THE 24-HOUR COMIC CHALLENGE WAS INVENTED IN 1990 BY SCOTT McCLOUD.

THE CHALLENGE IS TO CREATE 24 PAGES OF COMICS IN ONE 24-HOUR PERIOD.

AND AS IF THAT'S NOT HARD ENOUGH, YOU ARE SUPPOSED TO ALSO MAKE UP THE STORY AS YOU GO!

I FIRST HEARD ABOUT THE 24-HOUR COMIC CHALLENGE IN 2001...

I **IMMEDIATELY** LIKED THE IDEA.

THE CONCEPT OF EACH PAGE BEING **TIMED** REALLY APPEALED TO ME.

:10 :20
:30 :40
:50 :60

ONE PAGE PER HOUR

↑ 10 MINUTE PANELS

:15 :30
:45 :60

15 MINUTE → PANELS

I DREW MY FIRST 24-HOUR COMIC ON DECEMBER 19TH, 2001 FROM 12AM – 11:41PM. WHAT AN EXPERIENCE!

IT WAS **SO INCREDIBLE,** I DECIDED TO TRY AND DRAW A 24-HOUR COMIC ONCE A YEAR FOR THE REST OF MY LIFE !

SO FAR, I'M DOING PRETTY WELL... I'VE DONE NINE 24-HOUR COMICS IN NINE YEARS.

212 PAGES OF COMICS!

SOME OF THIS STUFF IS EVEN PRETTY GOOD!

THAT'S WHY I DECIDED TO MAKE **THIS BOOK.** TO COLLECT THE GOOD STUFF!

BUT AS SOON AS I DECIDED TO MAKE A COLLECTION OF 24-HOUR COMICS, I WAS CONFUSED ABOUT HOW TO DESIGN IT...

IT SEEMED **WRONG** SOMEHOW, TO SPEND A LOT OF TIME DRAWING A NICE COVER AND MAKING A CLEAN, POLISHED LAYOUT FOR THE BOOK.

BECAUSE THE **GUTS** OF THE BOOK WERE ALL DRAWN FRANTICALLY IN THE MIDDLE OF THE NIGHT, WITH THE CLOCK TICKING!

THAT'S WHEN IT CAME TO ME!

SNAP!

I'D **DESIGN** AND **LAYOUT** THE WHOLE BOOK IN 24 HOURS!

AND THAT'S WHAT I'M DOING, **RIGHT NOW!**

BEFORE EACH OF THE SIX 24-HOUR COMICS IN THIS BOOK, YOU'LL FIND A BRIEF INTRODUCTION, ON PAGES WITH THESE **BLACK GUTTERS**.

ALL OF THESE PAGES WERE DRAWN ON MARCH 21ST, 2010 AND I'M HOPING THERE WILL BE TWENTY-FOUR OF THEM, THUS MAKING IT A BOOK OF **SEVEN** 24-HOUR COMICS!

I'M ALSO GOING TO SCAN IN THE PAGES, LAY THEM OUT IN INDESIGN, DRAW THE COVER AND UPLOAD THE WHOLE THING TO LULU.COM BEFORE MY 24 HOURS ARE UP.

...OR AT LEAST I'M GOING TO **TRY** TO DO ALL THAT STUFF... I THINK I CAN GET IT ALL DONE!

I ALWAYS START MY 24-HOUR COMICS AT MIDNIGHT.

THAT WAY, I FINISH AT MIDNIGHT THE NEXT NIGHT AND I CAN JUST GO STRAIGHT TO SLEEP.

I ALSO LIKE THE PURITY OF STARTING THE PROJECT JUST AS A NEW DAY BEGINS. IT ALSO MAKES IT EASIER TO MARK MY PROGRESS.

3 AM

PAGE 3

BUT IT ALSO MEANS I START THE COMIC **TIRED** AND FINISH IT **REALLY TIRED**.

NOT SURPRISINGLY, **SLEEP** WAS THE THEME OF MY FIRST TWO 24-HOUR COMICS.

MY FIRST 24-HOUR COMIC, "SLEEP-LESS" IS ABOUT A COLLEGE STUDENT WHO TAKES A DRUG WHICH PREVENTS HIM FROM SLEEPING FOR THREE WHOLE MONTHS.

MY SECOND 24-HOUR COMIC, "SUPER-DREAM" THEN SHOWS THIS STUDENT'S PENT-UP DREAM ACTIVITY, WHICH WAS ALL BASED ON MY OWN REAL DREAMS.

MY THIRD 24-HOUR COMIC, "COLORS" WAS MORE EXPERIMENTAL. IT DEVOTED FOUR PAGES EACH TO THE COLORS RED, ORANGE, YELLOW, GREEN, BLUE AND PURPLE.

ALL THREE WERE TRUE, STREAM-OF-CONSCIOUSNESS 24-HOUR COMICS, AND THEY CAN ALL BE READ FOR FREE ON MY WEBSITE!

alec-longstreth.com

7

FOR MY **FOURTH** 24-HOUR COMIC, I WANTED TO TRY SOMETHING A LITTLE MORE... STRUCTURED.

I **KNEW** I COULD MAKE IT THROUGH THE CHALLENGE, SO I STARTED TREATING THE EXERCISE LIKE A TWENTY-FOUR HOUR **WORK** BLOCK.

I STILL DIDN'T WRITE ANYTHING DOWN BEFOREHAND...

BUT I DEFINITELY **THOUGHT** ABOUT THE STORIES I WAS GOING TO DRAW!

"SCARS" WAS DRAWN FROM 12AM - 11:57PM ON NOVEMBER 20TH, 2004. I HOPE YOU ENJOY IT!

8

SCARS

ALEC LONGSTRETH'S

november 20th, 2004 all day

[TABLE OF CONTENTS]

A 24 HOUR COMIC

HI! MY NAME IS ALEC LONGSTRETH.

I'VE BEEN DRAWING COMICS PRETTY SERIOUSLY NOW FOR ABOUT FOUR YEARS.

A LOT OF MY STORIES ARE "AUTOBIOGRAPHICAL."

SO I'M ALWAYS TRYING TO FIGURE OUT → WHAT ARE THE STORIES THAT ARE WORTH TELLING?

ESPECIALLY 'CAUSE COMICS TAKE SO LONG TO DRAW, I DON'T WANT TO WASTE MY TIME ON AN UNINTERESTING STORY.

OR **YOUR** TIME EITHER!

SO OVER THE YEARS I'VE COME UP WITH THIS RULE OF THUMB...

IF I'VE TOLD A STORY **THREE OR MORE TIMES** IN REAL LIFE THEN IT'S **COMICS WORTHY!**

AND ONE TYPE OF STORY I'VE TOLD HAS BEEN "COMICS WORTHY" FOR **YEARS**...

SCARS!

YEAH... IT SEEMS LIKE ALMOST **EVERY** SCAR HAS SOME SORT OF STORY BEHIND IT...

SO HERE ARE **MINE**, IN NO PARTICULAR ORDER!

SCAR #2

HAIRLINE

YES, BELIEVE IT OR NOT, **ANOTHER** FAMILY-INDUCED HEAD WOUND!

I GREW UP IN SEATTLE, WASHINGTON.

IN THE WINTER SOMETIMES MY FAMILY WOULD DRIVE UP INTO THE CASCADE MOUNTAINS...

TO GO **SLEDDING!**

THIS ONE YEAR, WHEN I WAS ABOUT **5**, WE GOT **SLEDS** FOR CHRISTMAS...

WHOA!

THE OLD-FASHION TYPE!

DADDY, AREN'T THOSE SLEDS **ILLEGAL** NOW BECAUSE THEY ARE **SO** DANGEROUS?

MOM

NONSENSE BRECKINRIDGE. THAT'S THE KIND OF SLED **I** HAD WHEN **I** WAS A BOY!

POP

MY DAD TOOK US UP TO THE MOUNTAINS TO TRY OUT OUR NEW SLEDS

WE PARKED WITH ALL THE OTHER CARS IN THE SKIING PARKING LOT.

WHUMP

THE SLEDDING AREA WAS OFF TO ONE SIDE OF THE SKIING AREA

THERE WERE A BUNCH OF **TEENAGERS** THERE.

C'MON ALEC!

GEE DAD... I DON'T KNOW...

13

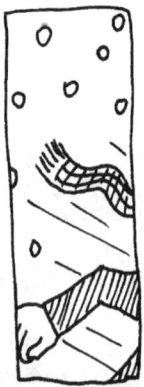

SCAR #3

LEFT KNUCKLES

MY **OTHER** SLEDDING SCAR HAPPENED RIGHT AT HOME

I DON'T REMEMBER HOW OLD I WAS, BUT GALEN WAS OLD ENOUGH TO BABYSIT ME.

WE WERE WATCHING "THE COSBY SHOW."

WHEN THE SHOW ENDED WE LOOKED OUTSIDE...

OH MY GOD! LOOK GALEN!

WE HADN'T EVEN NOTICED

IT **SNOWED!**

OH MY GOD! IT'S LIKE **TEN FEET** OF SNOW!

3"

CAN WE GO SLEDDING?

I THINK MOM WOULD SAY "YES".

GREEN

BUT MOM WOULD HAVE ALSO TOLD US TO WEAR OUR **GLOVES!**

WOO!

SLAM!

ALL OF THE NEIGHBORHOOD KIDS WERE SLEDDING TOO...

I KNOW! THERE'S **NO WAY** WE'LL HAVE SCHOOL TOMORROW!

I BORROWED SOMEONE'S DISH-SLED FOR A WHILE AND MADE A FEW RUNS DOWN OUR HILL

WOW! THANKS!

WHAT I **DIDN'T** REALIZE WAS THAT MY HAND WAS DRAGGING ACROSS THE PAVEMENT

IT WAS SO COLD THOUGH THAT MY HAND DIDN'T BLEED.

THAT WAS **SO** MUCH FUN!

15

OUR PARENTS WERE HOME BY THE TIME WE GOT BACK TO THE HOUSE.

THERE YOU ARE!

WE WENT SLEDDING

OF COURSE, IN THE WARM HOUSE MY HAND REALLY STARTED TO BLEED!

DO YOU THINK THERE WILL BE SCHOOL TOMORROW MOM?

≥GASP!≤

ALEC! WHAT DID YOU DO TO YOUR **HAND**?

I REMEMBER THINKING IT WAS COOL THAT I GOT TO WEAR A BAND AID ON EVERY FINGER

REALLY WHEN I THINK ABOUT IT, I THINK I DID ALRIGHT, IF THOSE WERE THE ONLY SCARS FROM MY CHILDHOOD.

YEAH, BY THE TIME I GOT MY NEXT SCAR **I** WAS OLD ENOUGH TO BABYSIT!

SCAR #4

LEFT PALM

IN FACT, THAT'S BASICALLY WHAT I WAS DOING!

AT ABOUT 16 I HAD REACHED THE RANK OF "CAMPER LEADER" AT HIDDEN VALLEY CAMP

I WAS ON AN OVERNIGHT HIKE WITH ONE OF THE YOUNGER BOYS GROUPS.

ROCK ISLAND

THEY WERE **SO** YOUNG IN FACT, THAT THEIR COUNSELOR HAD CONFISCATED ALL OF THEIR POCKET KNIVES FOR THE TRIP.

THAT WAY NO ONE WOULD BE IN DANGER OF HURTING THEMSELVES...

OF COURSE THIS WAS NOT WHAT THE KNIFE-CRAZED EIGHT YEAR OLDS WANTED TO HEAR.

AND SO, FRUSTRATED, I GRABBED THE STICK WITH BOTH HANDS... WHILE STILL HOLDING THE KNIFE!

!?!

IT WAS LIKE A GIANT SPRING

RRRRG!

SNAP!

FUCK!!!

UH... HEH! I MEAN... "OH DRAT!"

I HAD PUT THE KNIFE MOST OF THE WAY THROUGH MY HAND...

shplch

IF YOU THINK THAT'S GROSS THEN BEWARE OF THE NEXT ONE, WHICH IS EASILY MY WEIRDEST SCAR...

SCAR #5

TOUNGE

ABOUT HALF WAY THROUGH MY JUNIOR YEAR IN HIGH SCHOOL I DEVELOPED A STRANGE BUMP ON THE UNDERSIDE OF MY TONGUE

WHAT IS THAT UNDER THERE?

IT GOT BIGGER AND BIGGER UNTIL IT WAS REALLY STARTING TO GROSS ME OUT.

blech!

THEY DON'T EVEN **TRY** TO LIE TO YOU! (YOU KNOW: "THIS WON'T HURT TOO MUCH").

MR. LONGSTRETH THIS NEXT PART IS PRETTY... **UNPLEASANT**...

≥GULP≤

HAVE I MENTIONED THAT I **HATE** NEEDLES???

BUT IT IS **VERY** IMPORTANT THAT YOU **DON'T MOVE**

I START CRYING AS THE FIRST NEEDLE ENTERS MY TONGUE

FIRST THEY GO IN AT THE TIP UNTIL THEY ARE OVER THE MUCOSEAL

THEN **AGAIN** FROM THE SIDE

THE REST IS QUICK, PAINLESS AND **SURREAL**

HE'S TYING **STRING** INTO MY **TONGUE**!

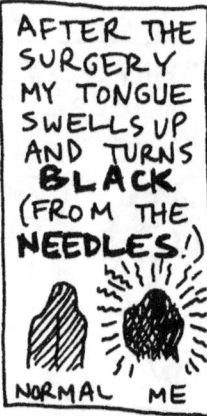

AFTER THE SURGERY MY TONGUE SWELLS UP AND TURNS **BLACK** (FROM THE **NEEDLES**!)

NORMAL   ME

I CAN'T TALK FOR A WEEK, BUT IT'S OKAY. I HAVE PLENTY TO THINK ABOUT!

I AM NEVER LETTING **ANYONE** PUT ANOTHER GODDAMNED NEEDLE IN ME.

AND TO THIS DAY I HAVE A LITTLE CROSS SHAPED SCAR UNDER MY TONGUE. IT'S WEIRD 'CAUSE I CAN'T **TASTE** OR **FEEL** WITH THAT PART!

BRRRR! LET'S TRY SOMETHING A LITTLE MORE **MELLOW** NOW, EH?

SCAR #6

LEFT PALM

ONE NIGHT IN HIGH SCHOOL I DECIDED TO EAT A BROWNIE.

HMMMmm

MY MOM HAD MADE THE BROWNIES A WHILE AGO. THEY HAD BEEN SITTING IN THE KITCHEN

IT WAS DARK IN THE KITCHEN

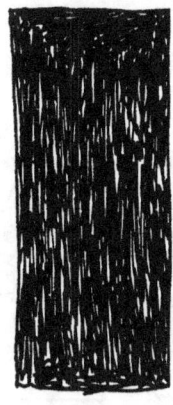

ANYWAYS, claire AND I USED TO JOKE THAT I WAS VEER'S PSYCHOTIC STALKER...

AND THAT I WAS TRYING TO SPELL HIS NAME ON MY HAND WITH CUTS... **VERY SLOWLY.**

UNFORTUNATELY I HAVEN'T EVEN BEGUN THE FIRST "E" AND I THINK VEER DIED WHILE I WAS AT COLLEGE...

SCAR #7

STOMACH

claire ACTUALLY CAME ON THE TRIP WHERE I GOT MY NEXT SCAR...

SHE AND MY FAMILY ALL SPENT A WEEK OUT AT THE OREGON COAST.

THIS ONE DAY MY DAD AND I DECIDED TO FLY A KITE.

OKAY! GO!

IT WAS A **REALLY** WINDY DAY!

WOO!

THE KITE WAS ALMOST PULLING MY DAD ALONG.

WHOA.

HMMM...

ALEC! I DON'T THINK IT'S GOING TO H※

BUT THEN, JUST AS HE WAS TRYING TO WARN ME, THE KITE STRING SNAPPED!

HALF OF THE KITE STRING WENT WITH THE KITE... WE'RE FREE!

AND THE OTHER HALF (STILL ATTACHED TO THE SPOOL) BEGAN TO DRIFT BACK TO THE GROUND.

AS SOME SORT OF REFLEX I TOOK OFF AFTER THE KITE...

AND BY SOME WEIRD TWIST OF FATE THE SPOOL-END OF THE KITE-STRING DRIFTED DOWN RIGHT IN FRONT OF ME...

RIGHT AS MY DAD YANKED BACK ON THE SPOOL! RRG!

AHHH! ZZZ!

YOU WOULDN'T THINK KITE STRING COULD DO MUCH DAMAGE, BUT THE CUT (OR BURN?) WAS SUPRISINGLY DEEP. AND WITH THE SALTY OCEAN AIR IT WAS PRETTY UNCOMFORTABLE. IT STINGS! SORRY...

EVENTUALLY WE FOUND THE KITE... HERE IT IS! NO! LEAVE ME BE!

THE STRING ON IT WAS SO TANGLED UP. WE CAN JUST CUT THAT OFF. NO.

WHAT DO YOU MEAN, "NO"? IT'LL COST US $3.00 FOR SOME NEW STRING! NO

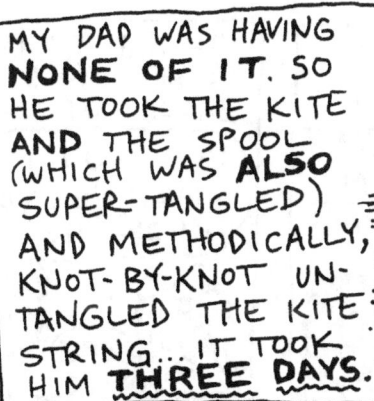

MY DAD WAS HAVING NONE OF IT. SO HE TOOK THE KITE AND THE SPOOL (WHICH WAS ALSO SUPER-TANGLED) AND METHODICALLY, KNOT-BY-KNOT UNTANGLED THE KITE STRING... IT TOOK HIM THREE DAYS.

(MY MOM TOLD ME LATER HE HAD MIGRAINES FOR THE WHOLE TRIP...)

IT'S FUNNY THAT IN THE BEGINNING OF THIS I SAID "IN NO PARTICULAR ORDER."

BECAUSE REALLY, SO FAR IT'S BEEN **CHRONOLOGICAL** (MOSTLY).

SO.. I GUESS I'LL JUST CONTINUE WITH THAT...

EVER SINCE I WENT TO COLLEGE IT SEEMS LIKE THE ONLY PLACE I GET NEW SCARS IS AT **WORK**.

SCAR #8

RIGHT MIDDLE FINGER

I CAME HOME TO SEATTLE AFTER MY FIRST YEAR OF COLLEGE TO WORK...

UGH... Ooo

Seattle Times Classified

SOMEHOW I GOT HOOKED UP WITH THIS YOUTH CENTER. THE GUY SAID HE WOULD LOOK FOR SOME WORK FOR ME EVEN THOUGH I WAS OVER 18.

THANKS!

NO SWEAT.

HE FOUND ME A JOB FOR A WEEK WORKING AT A SMALL PRINTING COMPANY

YOU ALEC?

YES SIR.

WELCOME.

IT WAS A LOT OF FOLDING, STAPLING ETC.

CLICK

ON MY SECOND-TO-LAST DAY THEY PAIRED ME WITH THIS **REALLY** OBNOXIOUS WOMAN.

I'M WITH **HIM**? GREAAAT...

?

WE HAD TO PUT TOGETHER SOME BROCHURE...

I'LL RUN THE MACHINE, YOU PACK THEM, K?

SURE

PRESS

YOU WOULD THINK OPERATING TABLE SAWS AND POWER TOOLS ALL DAY WOULD SUPPLY **LOTS** OF SCARS...

BUT **MOST** OF THE PLACES I'VE WORKED HAVE BEEN **VERY** SAFETY-CONSCIOUS.

I ONLY HAVE THREE SCARS FROM MY THEATRE WORK...

SCAR #9

TOP OF HEAD

WE WERE DOING THE SET FOR THIS NEW OPERA "COYOTE TALES" AND MIKE GRUBE DESIGNS IT WITH ALL **CIRCULAR** PLATFORMS

WAIT, IS THIS A JOKE?

TO MAKE MATTERS WORSE WE HAVE TO LIFT AN ACTOR 15' IN THE AIR **ONSTAGE** SO RICK IS BUILDING A **GIANT** SEE-SAW.

(PULLED FROM PIT)

15'

20'?

IT WASN'T A DAY I USUALLY WORKED BUT RICK ASKED ME TO COME IN AND DO SOME WELDING

MORNING J.V.

ALEC!

I'LL BE WELDING

I AM A MORON

CLUNK

THE BASEMENT DOOR IS ALWAYS LOCKED IN THE MORNING.

HMM... NO J.V.

THE LIGHTBRIDGE WAS IN SO THE ELECTRICIANS COULD HANG SOME LIGHTS.

HEY JEN, CAN I GET THE KEY TO THE BASEMENT, I'M SUPPOSED TO WELD FOR RICK.

BRING IT BACK.

26

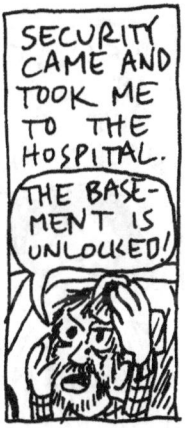

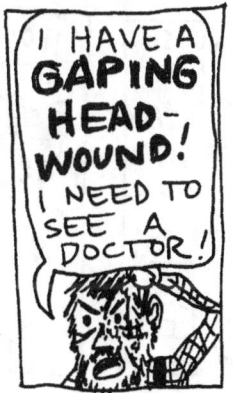

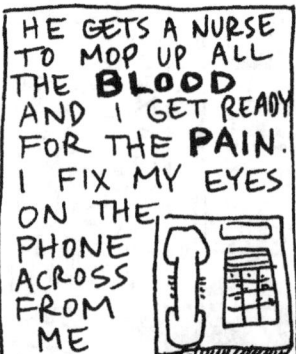

THE STAPLES DEFINITELY HURT MORE THAN THE LIGHT!

IT'S PRETTY COOL HAVING STAPLES IN YOUR HEAD THOUGH... YOU FEEL LIKE FRANKENSTEIN'S MONSTER!

Gragh!

THE MAIN DOWNSIDE WAS NOT BEING ABLE TO WASH MY HAIR FOR 2 WEEKS. YUCK!

AND NOW, WHEN I SHAVE MY HEAD I HAVE A COOL LINE THERE.

NO BEARD EITHER!

SCAR #10

LEFT INDEX KNUCKLE

THERE'S ACTUALLY NOT MUCH OF A STORY ABOUT THIS ONE... I WAS WORKING IN THE UW SCENE SHOP...

CHUGGA CHUGGA CHUGGA CHUGGA CHUGGA CHUGGA

I WASN'T PAYING CLOSE ENOUGH ATTENTION TO THE DRUM SANDER...

UGA GGA UGA GGA UGA GA

CHU CHU CHU CHU CHU

AND POOF! A MOMENT OF ZONING OUT AND I'M SCARRED FOR LIFE!

OW!

SO PAY ATTENTION WHEN YOU ARE USING POWER TOOLS!

SCAR #11

LEFT ARM

ALAN GAVE ME AN IMPORTANT WELD...

THESE PICK POINTS ARE GOING TO SUPPORT THE WHOLE UNIT, SO MAKE SURE YOU GET A GOOD WELD.

RIGHT.

HMMM... IT'LL BE TRICKIER TO WELD UPSIDE-DOWN BUT AT LEAST WE WON'T HAVE TO STAND THIS UP!

29

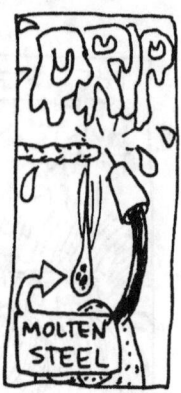

HA HA HA! I ALWAYS THOUGHT THAT ABRUPT ENDING WAS PRETTY FUNNY.

"SCARS" WAS MY FIRST **GAIMAN*** **VARIATION** 24-HOUR COMIC, WHICH MEANS THAT I GOT TO 24 HOURS AND STOPPED, EVEN THOUGH I DIDN'T HAVE 24 PAGES.

ONLY 21

*NAMED AFTER NEIL GAIMAN

AND MY **NEXT** 24-HOUR COMIC WAS AN **EASTMAN*** **VARIATION**, BECAUSE I KEPT DRAWING UNTIL IT WAS DONE, EVEN THOUGH IT TOOK MORE THAN 24 HOURS.

*NAMED AFTER KEVIN EASTMAN

IT WAS ALSO MY FIRST **COLLABORATIVE** 24-HOUR COMIC. I DREW THE WHOLE THING WITH MY GOOD PAL **AARON RENIER**.

31

2005 WAS AN EXTREMELY BUSY YEAR FOR ME, BECAUSE I HAD GONE BACK TO SCHOOL AT PRATT INSTITUTE.

I ACTUALLY DIDN'T MANAGE TO DRAW A 24-HOUR COMIC DURING THE CALENDAR YEAR OF 2005. I HAD TOO MUCH OTHER STUFF GOING ON...

BUT AARON AND I ONLY MISSED IT BY A COUPLE OF DAYS! WE SAT DOWN TO DRAW OUR COLLABORATIVE 24-HOUR COMIC ON JANUARY 2ND, 2006.

IN RETROSPECT, IT MIGHT NOT HAVE BEEN THE BEST DAY FOR THE PROJECT...

AARON HAD BEEN OUT AT A NEW YEAR'S EVE PARTY UNTIL THE WEE HOURS OF JANUARY 1ST. HE GOT A FEW HOURS OF SLEEP AND THEN I FORCED HIM TO START DRAWING AT MIDNIGHT. POOR AARON!

YOU READY?!

WE PASSED THE PAGES BACK AND FORTH, SO THAT WE BOTH DREW IN EVERY SINGLE PANEL. WE MADE UP THE STORY AS WE WENT, WHICH WAS TONS OF FUN. IT WAS GOING GREAT UNTIL HOUR 17...

:SIGH:

I COULD TELL AARON WAS REALLY RUNNING OUT OF STEAM. I WAS WORRIED HE MIGHT EVEN THROW IN THE TOWEL!

UGGH... ALEC?

YEAH?

:GULP:

I NEED TO GO GET SOME **COFFEE.**

OH! PHEW! YEAH, OKAY, LET'S GO!

HEAVILY CAFFEINATED, WE BOTH MADE IT THROUGH THE HOME STRETCH. IT WAS 24 HOURS AND 51 MINUTES ALL TOGETHER.

HA HA HA HA HA

AARON IS A MUCH MORE SKILLED CARTOONIST THAN I AM, AND IT WAS A REAL HONOR TO GET TO DRAW ON THE SAME BRISTOL AS HIM FOR A DAY.

I LEARNED MORE ABOUT DRAWING WITH A BRUSH **ON** THAT ONE DAY THAN I DID THE WHOLE **YEAR** LEADING UP TO IT.

OKAY, WELL, I HOPE YOU ENJOY OUR STORY, "CRISPY GINGER CRUMPLES!"

Crispy Ginger Crumples

A 24-HOUR COMIC
BY
ALEC LONGSTRETH
&
AARON RENIER

DRAWN **ALL** DAY — JAN. 2ND, 2006

ZORCH... I LEFT MY PICK-AXE BACK IN MY CELL! I NEED TO GO BACK...

PROGIE... WE'RE NOT GOING TO THE SPICE MINES...

WE'RE HEADING TO NORTHOS...LAND OF BOILING LEAD!

38

39

40

45

47

50

55

58

ALL OF THE COMICS YOU'VE READ SO FAR WERE POSTED ON MY WEBSITE, THE DAY AFTER THEY WERE COMPLETED.

THIS NEXT ONE **WASN'T**.

≡CLICK≡

I'VE NEVER RELEASED MY SIXTH 24-HOUR COMIC **ANYWHERE**. USUALLY I SAY IT'S BECAUSE THE STORY IS "TOO PERSONAL"

IT MIGHT BE MORE ACCURATE TO SAY IT'S TOO **CREEPY**...

WHEN I DREW THE COMIC IN 2006, I WAS EXTREMELY... WELL, **LONELY**.

IT HAD BEEN ABOUT **FOUR YEARS** SINCE I HAD DATED ANYONE. I WENT ON A FEW "DATES" IN NEW YORK, BUT HATED EVERY SECOND OF THE PROCESS.

bla bla la bla bla bla bla bla

UGGH! GET ME **OUT** OF HERE!

I WANTED TO **SKIP** THE WHOLE DATING PROCESS AND JUST ALREADY **BE** WITH SOME GREAT GIRL.

THAT'S WHEN I HAD ONE OF MY STRANGER COMICS IDEAS... I COULD JUST **INVENT** A GIRLFRIEND COMICS **CHARACTER**.

EVERYONE HATED THIS IDEA

YOU KNOW, INSTEAD OF HAVING TO **GO** ON A DATE, I COULD JUST **DRAW** US GOING ON A DATE. IT WOULD PROBABLY TAKE ABOUT THE SAME AMOUNT OF TIME!

ALEC, **NO.**

THE **LAST** THING YOU NEED RIGHT NOW IS ANOTHER REASON TO STAY IN YOUR WINDOWLESS APARTMENT, DRAWING. YOU NEED TO GET OUTSIDE **MORE.**

GOOD ADVICE

BUT I IGNORED THE ADVICE OF MY FRIENDS AND WENT AHEAD AND DESIGNED MY SKETCHBOOK GIRLFRIEND, WHO I NAMED **SUSANNE,** AFTER MY FAVORITE WEEZER SONG.

FOR YEARS I HAD BEEN DRAWING (AND NUMBERING) LITTLE DAYDREAMS IN MY SKETCHBOOKS. I DECIDED MY NEXT 24-HOUR COMIC WOULD BE THE 7TH DAYDREAM IN THE SERIES.

I **UNDERSTAND** THAT THE WHOLE CREATE-YOUR-OWN GIRLFRIEND THING IS TOTALLY CREEPY!

IF IT'S ANY CONSOLATION, THE 24-HOUR COMIC IS THE ONLY THING I EVER DREW SUSANNE IN. I THINK IT GOT HER OUT OF MY SYSTEM.

STILL, I MUST ADMIT... IT WAS SORT OF BLISSFUL, GETTING LOST IN A DAYDREAM FOR A WHOLE DAY.

I CONSTRUCTED A NON-EXISTENT TIME AND PLACE, WHERE ALL OF MY CLOSEST FRIENDS LIVED IN ONE TOWN AND I WAS A SUCCESSFUL CARTOONIST, SUPPORTING MYSELF WITH MY ART.

I GUESS **THAT'S** THE MOST EMBARRASSING PART OF THIS WHOLE STORY — SO OPENLY SHOWING WHAT IT IS THAT I **WANT.**

WELL, **ANYWAY,** THIS STORY HAS BEEN A SKELETON IN MY CLOSET FOR LONG ENOUGH! IT'S TIME TO PUT IT IN PRINT, SO I CAN PUT IT BEHIND ME.

SO FOR BETTER OR WORSE, HERE'S "DAYDREAM #0007" WHICH WAS DRAWN FROM MIDNIGHT TO MIDNIGHT ON MAY 18TH, 2006.

I HOPE IT DOESN'T **CREEP** YOU OUT TOO MUCH!

DAYDREAM

#0007

a 24-hour comic
by ALEC LONGSTRETH

69

I'M SO PROUD OF YOU ALEC.

ALL OF YOUR HARD WORK REALLY PAID OFF.

83

84

OKAY! LET'S KEEP MOVING! WE STILL HAVE THREE MORE 24-HOUR COMICS!

THE NEXT ONE KIND OF HAS ITS OWN INTRO, SO I DON'T REALLY NEED TO SET IT UP...

JUST DON'T GET CONFUSED! BLACK GUTTERS AND CRAZY BEARD EQUALS **2010** ALEC.

THAT NEATLY TRIMMED VERSION OF ME WAS DRAWN FROM MIDNIGHT ON SEPTEMBER 26TH, 2007 TO 2:08AM ON THE 27TH

AS I SIT DOWN TO DRAW THIS STORY, IT IS SEPTEMBER 26TH, 2007. **ONE DAY** BEFORE MY BEST FRIEND GABE MOVES TO NEW YORK CITY.

I HAVE KNOWN GABE ALMOST **TEN YEARS** NOW...

AND IN THAT TIME WE HAVE HAD A LOT OF UPS AND DOWNS. IT HAS NOT ALWAYS BEEN AN EASY FRIENDSHIP.

BUT THROUGH IT ALL I HAVE ALWAYS CONSIDERED GABE MY CLOSEST FRIEND. EVEN WHEN I FELT LIKE STRANGLING HIM!

I GUESS I JUST WANTED TO SPEND THIS DAY REFLECTING UPON MY FRIENDSHIP WITH GABE AND ITS CURRENT STATE BEFORE HE MOVES HERE AND IT CHANGES YET AGAIN.

IT ALL BEGAN AT **OBERLIN COLLEGE** IN 1998...

91

MY DAD AND I DROVE INTO TOWN ON A STICKY OHIO AUGUST NIGHT.

MY DAD HAD TO LEAVE FOR A CONFERENCE THE NEXT DAY. HE HUNG AROUND JUST LONG ENOUGH TO ACCOMPLISH THREE THINGS:

HE GOT ME SITU-ATED IN MY DORM ROOM.

HE HELPED ME SET UP MY BANK ACCOUNT IN TOWN.

HE BOUGHT ME A COMPUTER.

THANKS FOR EVERYTHING DAD.

I LOVE YOU. LEARN LOTS.

DON'T FORGET, THIS WAS 1998: THE YEAR OF THE VERY FIRST iMac!!!

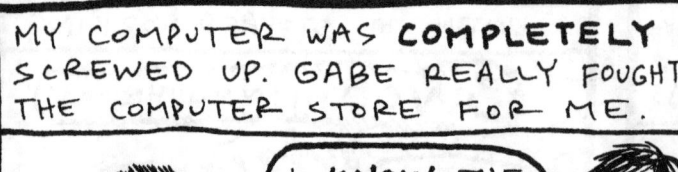

MY COMPUTER WAS **COMPLETELY** SCREWED UP. GABE REALLY FOUGHT THE COMPUTER STORE FOR ME.

I **KNOW** THE iMACS ARE SUPPOSED TO BE FLAWLESS, BUT I'M TELLING YOU, THIS ONE'S A **LEMON!**

HE CONVINCED THEM TO GIVE ME A NEW iMAC.

THANKS GABE! I OWE YOU ONE!

AS MY FIRST YEAR PROGRESSED, I QUICKLY LEARNED THAT MY **ROOMMATE** WAS ONE OF THE MOST HORRIBLE HUMAN BEINGS I HAVE EVER MET.

SEXIST, RACIST "JOKE"

ONE NIGHT, I COULDN'T STAND TO BE IN THE SAME ROOM WITH HIM FOR ANOTHER MINUTE, I HATED HIM SO MUCH.

HEY, WOULD IT BE OKAY IF I STUDIED IN HERE WITH YOU?

SURE! COME ON IN!

AND SO I BEGAN HANGING OUT IN GABE'S ROOM... **A LOT.**

GABE AND I WERE ALSO "ON THE SAME PAGE" ABOUT MOST ASPECTS OF COLLEGE LIFE.

NAMELY, WE GAVE VERY LITTLE IMPORTANCE TO THINGS LIKE **SLEEP** AND **PERSONAL HYGENE.**

JESUS! I **STINK**!

WHEN WAS THE LAST TIME YOU TOOK A SHOWER?

LET'S SEE... SUNDAY, MONDAY... TUESDAY... THREE? FOUR DAYS? I GUESS TONIGHT'S THE NIGHT!

SNIFF UM... MAYBE **I** SHOULD TAKE A SHOWER TOO!

AND SO SOMETIMES GABE AND I WOULD SHOWER AT THE SAME TIME.

OFF TO TAKE A SHOWER WITH YOUR BOYFRIEND?

"HA.HA."

TAKING A SHOWER IS A GREAT TIME TO TALK. IT WAS ALWAYS VERY RELAXING....

SINCE GABE AND I WERE FROM THE SAME REGION OF THE U.S.A. WE ALSO HAD A SIMILAR APPRECIATION OF THE OHIO WEATHER.

HOLY CRAP!

LOOK HOW HARD IT'S SNOWING!!!

I WONDER IF ANY ONE ELSE IS AWAKE TO SEE THIS...

WE SHOULD FIND SOME PEOPLE TO HAVE A SNOWBALL FIGHT WITH!

WE WANDERED UP TO NORTH CAMPUS, FIGURING WE'D RUN INTO **SOMEONE** ALONG THE WAY.

NICE...HUH...HUH... SNOW...HUH...MAN!

I AGREE! HIS NAME IS "ED". I'M MAKING HIM A NAME TAG OUT OF SNOW.

LOOK OUT ED! THE SUN IS RISING!! IT'S GOING TO **MELT** YOU!!!

WOW. MAYBE WE SHOULD GET BACK TO OUR HOMEWORK...

UH... YEAH.

GABE AND I HAD MANY OTHER ADVENTURES THAT YEAR, AND BY THE END OF IT, OUR FRIENDSHIP WAS SOLIDIFIED.

ONE OF THE STRANGER THINGS ABOUT MY FRIENDSHIP WITH GABE IS THAT WE **FIGHT**.

DO YOU EVEN UNDERSTAND THE AMOUNT OF PRESSURE GENERATED AT THOSE DEPTHS?!

SOMETIMES ABOUT THE STUPIDEST THINGS!

OF COURSE IT WOULD CRUSH A SODA BOTTLE!

I HAVE ALWAYS SEEN THIS AS A SIGN OF OUR CLOSENESS. WE KNOW WE CAN ARGUE AND BLOW OFF SOME STEAM WITHOUT JEOPARDIZING OUR FRIENDSHIP. LIKE SIBLINGS.

MY **SOPHOMORE** YEAR, I LIVED WITH GABE AND OUR FRIENDS FRUNCH & SAM. I WAS A LITTLE WORRIED ABOUT OUR ARGUMENTS....

NOW LISTEN GABE.

IT SEEMS INEVITABLE THAT AT **SOME** POINT THIS YEAR WE ARE GOING TO GET IN A FIGHT.

AGREED.

SO TO HELP DIFUSE THE SITUATION, I HEREBY GIVE YOU PERMISSION TO THROW ONE FULL GLASS OF WATER IN MY FACE AND I PROMISE **NOT** TO GET ANGRY.

DEAL.

ARGUABLY OUR WORST FIGHT EVER WAS THE "TETRIS FIGHT."

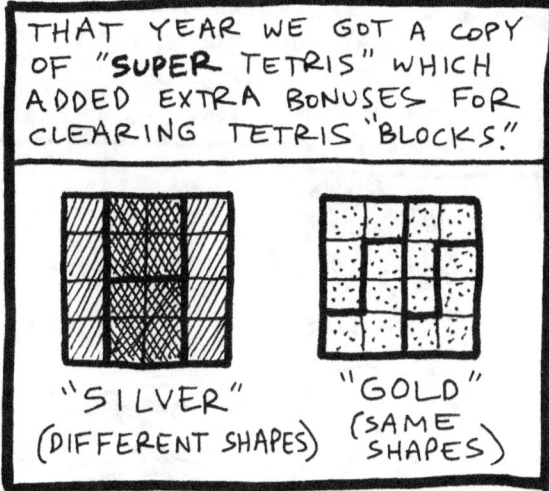

THAT YEAR WE GOT A COPY OF "**SUPER** TETRIS" WHICH ADDED EXTRA BONUSES FOR CLEARING TETRIS "BLOCKS."

"SILVER"
(DIFFERENT SHAPES)

"GOLD"
(SAME SHAPES)

OUR QUAD BECAME **OBSESSED** WITH THIS GAME. I WAS THE WORST AT IT AND GABE WAS THE BEST. HE WAS **REALLY REALLY** GOOD AT IT....

FRUNCH, WANNA COME WITH ME TO THE APOLLO?

ISN'T IT THAT CHICK FLICK WITH SUSAN SURANDON?

YEAH, AND **NATALIE PORTMAN**.

HUP!

GABE. NEW NATALIE PORTMAN MOVIE.

NAW MAN, I JUST STARTED A GAME OF SUPER TETRIS.

FRUNCH AND I WALKED TO THE MOVIE, WATCHED IT AND WALKED BACK. WHEN WE RE-ENTERED THE QUAD OVER **THREE HOURS** LATER, GABE WAS STILL PLAYING THE **SAME GAME**.

NO WAY!

THE PIECES ARE **BLURS!**

105

GABE WAS UNDER **A LOT** OF PRESSURE. IT WAS ONLY A MATTER OF TIME UNTIL HE CRACKED...

≥TWITCH≤
≥TWITCH≤
≥TWITC
≥TW

THEN, IT HAPPENED!

OH NO!

OH, YOU SHOULD HAVE MOVED THAT ONE TO THE LEFT.

LONGSTRETH, YOU **SUCK** AT THIS GAME! DON'T TELL ME HOW TO PLAY !!!

WE YELLED BACK AND FORTH FOR A WHILE, FINALLY STOPPING AFTER GABE SHOVED THE CONTROLLER IN MY FACE, SCREAMING

YOU WANNA PLAY?! YOU WON'T LAST **FIVE** <u>MINUTES</u>!

WE TRIED TO TURN TO FRUNCH AS AN IMPARTIAL JUDGE, BUT HE DIDN'T GROW UP WITH SISTERS OR BROTHERS AND HE SEEMED FLUSTERED BY ALL OF THE YELLING...

I COULDN'T TELL! IT... IT HAPPENED TOO FAST!

BUT PERHAPS THE "GHOST BUSTERS" FIGHT WAS EVEN **WORSE.**

AT THE TIME, GABE HAD NEVER SEEN THE FILM "GHOSTBUSTERS."

YOU'VE GOT TO BE KIDDING ME!

I TRACKED DOWN A COPY OF THE MOVIE AND THEN INVITED A BUNCH OF OUR FRIENDS OVER TO WATCH IT.

GABE'S **NEVER** SEEN IT. CAN YOU BELIEVE THAT?!

OKAY, ARE WE READY?

HEY WAIT! WHERE'S **GABE?**

I'M IN HERE.

WELL COME ON GABE! WE'RE READY TO START!

UH...MAYBE YOU SHOULD START WITHOUT ME. I NEED TO FINISH THIS PAPER.

WE HAD NOT SPOKEN ABOUT THE ARRANGEMENT IN SEVEN MONTHS. I HAD FORGOTTEN IT COMPLETELY.

EVEN THOUGH GABE WAS JOKING ABOUT THE FIGHT STUFF, HE **DID** FALL FAST ASLEEP HALF WAY THROUGH "GHOSTBUSTERS."

SEVEN
YEARS
LATER
IN
NEW
YORK
CITY...

SO JIM AND I SET UP THIS DEAL WHERE WE CAN THROW A FULL GLASS OF WATER IN THE OTHER'S FACE ONCE A YEAR AND YOU CAN'T GET MAD.

CAROLYN

...SO THEN JIM THREW IT ALL INTO MY FACE. RIGHT IN FRONT OF EVERYONE!

?

OH COME ON! THAT'S HILARIOUS!

IT **IS** HILARIOUS, BUT NOT FOR THE REASONS YOU ARE THINKING OF....

THAT WAS YOU AND GABE?

...DAMN.

MY JUNIOR YEAR WAS GABE'S SENIOR YEAR. WE LIVED AT OPPOSITE ENDS OF CAMPUS AND RARELY HUNG OUT.

MOSTLY WE'D SEE EACHOTHER IN SCHOOL ACTIVITIES. WE WERE BOTH ON THE STUDENT THEATRE ASSOCIATION BOARD.

I HELPED BUILD THE SET FOR GABE'S SENIOR PLAY.

SOMETIMES WE WOULD THROW TOGETHER A SCENE OR ONE-ACT FOR AD-HOC THEATRE SLOTS.

WE CHOREOGRAPHED A FIGHT SCENE FOR OUR STAGE COMBAT CLASS.

KI-YA!

UF!

AFTER HIS GRADUATION WE DROVE FROM OHIO BACK TO PORTLAND... THE LONG WAY! *

* SEE PHASE 7 #003

111

MY SENIOR YEAR GABE WAS GONE.

OVER THE NEXT FEW YEARS I SAW GABE VERY SPORADICALLY. HE VISITED OBERLIN TWICE MY SENIOR YEAR: FOR A WEDDING AND FOR STAR WARS.

THE EPISODE II LINE STARTS HERE

WHEN I MOVED TO L.A. AFTER GRADUATING, HE TURNED UP ONE WEEKEND TO COMPETE IN A MAGIC TOURNAMENT.

I WON $600!

WHAT?! DINNER'S ON YOU!

I'D ALSO SEE HIM AT HIS ANNUAL NEW YEAR'S EVE PARTIES IN PORTLAND.

GRIZZO

THEN, IN 2004 I MOVED TO PORTLAND TO LIVE WITH FRUNCH & GWYN.

I NAIVELY ASSUMED THAT GABE AND I WOULD FALL BACK INTO OUR OLD FRIENDSHIP SINCE WE WERE BOTH IN THE SAME TOWN AGAIN.

HEY GABE, IT'S ALEC! WANNA HANG OUT TONIGHT?

BUT A LOT CAN CHANGE IN THOSE FIRST FEW YEARS AFTER COLLEGE.

UM... I'M GOING TO THE BAR WITH SOME OF THE GUYS, BUT YOU ARE WELCOME TO JOIN US.

GABE OBVIOUSLY ALREADY HAD A NETWORK OF FRIENDS WHEN I MOVED TO TOWN AND OUR INTERESTS DIDN'T USUALLY OVERLAP.

BLAZERS

BEER

AT ONE POINT WHILE I WAS LIVING IN PORTLAND I WENT A WHOLE **MONTH** WITHOUT SEEING GABE.

WELL I GUESS WE ARE BOTH JUST REALLY BUSY.

I GUESS...

I GOT REALLY FRUSTRATED WITH GABE. HE IS **SUCH** A CREATIVE, INTELLIGENT PERSON AND IT SEEMED TO ME THAT HE WAS NOT UTILIZING THOSE TRAITS IN EITHER HIS WORK OR HIS FREE TIME.

MR. JUDGEMENTAL

ALSO HE WAS DATING THIS **AWFUL** GIRL WHO WAS MAKING HIM COMPLETELY **MISERABLE.**

WHY DON'T YOU BREAK UP WITH HER GABE???

IT'S NOT THAT SIMPLE LONGSTRETH!

IN SOME WAYS, IT WAS A BIT OF A RELIEF WHEN I LEFT PORTLAND AND MOVED TO NEW YORK.

SINCE THEN, GABE HAS HAD A LOT OF CHANGES IN HIS LIFE.

HE BROKE UP WITH THE GIRL, LEFT HIS JOB TO TRAVEL THE WORLD FOR A YEAR, TOOK SOME FILM COURSES AND IS MAKING A DOCUMENTARY ABOUT MAGIC IN HIS SPARE TIME.

I HAVE MADE SOME CHANGES ALSO.

I DATED A CREEPILY SIMILAR GIRL (AND NOW EMPATHIZE WITH GABE'S PLIGHTS BACK IN PORTLAND) ALSO I STARTED **DRINKING**, WHICH MAKES IT EASIER TO HANG OUT WITH GABE.

NOW MY FRIENDSHIP WITH GABE FEELS AS STRONG AS IT EVER HAS. I'M REALLY LOOKING FORWARD TO LIVING IN NEW YORK WITH HIM!

NO DOUBT THERE WILL BE MORE ADVENTURES SOON. UNTIL THEN!

114

I WAS **RIGHT!** GABE AND I **DID** HAVE MANY ADVENTURES TOGETHER IN NEW YORK.

WE FOUND A COCKROACH INFESTED APARTMENT IN BROOKLYN, WHERE I HAPPILY SPENT MY LAST FEW MONTHS IN NEW YORK CITY.

GOOD NIGHT ALEC.

GOOD NIGHT GABE.

THEN I MOVED TO **VERMONT,** WHICH IS WHAT THE NEXT 24-HOUR COMIC IS ABOUT.

IT WILL ALSO EXPLAIN WHY I CURRENTLY LOOK LIKE A FREAKIN' **SASQUATCH!**

:SIGH:

ANYWAY, THIS 24-HOUR COMIC ALSO DOUBLED AS A BONUS MAIL TREAT FOR THE **PHASE 7 SUBSCRIBERS!**

IT WAS DRAWN ON SEPTEMBER 2ND, 2008 FROM 12:01AM TO 8:30PM, MY FASTEST 24-HOUR COMIC EVER!

OKAY, CHECK IT OUT!

The 2008 PHASE 7 SUMMER SUPPLEMENT

A 24-HOUR COMIC

by

ALEC LONGSTRETH

I CONSTANTLY WORRY ABOUT THE PHASE 7 SUBSCRIBERS.

THEY'RE WAITING!

MY FRIEND AUSTIN THINKS THIS IS PRETTY FUNNY.

OH, COME **ON** ALEC, IT'S NOT LIKE PEOPLE ARE GOING

WHERE **IS** THE NEW ISSUE OF **PHASE 7**?!

I KNOW HE'S PROBABLY RIGHT, BUT STILL I FEEL BAD ABOUT THE LONG WAIT BETWEEN ISSUES.

PHASE 7

#013

MARCH 2008

ALE LONGSTREH

118

ESPECIALLY **THIS** TIME, AS I'M TRYING TO FINISH THE NEXT CHAPTER OF MY ADVENTURE STORY, **BASEWOOD.**

THE FIRST CHAPTER TOOK ME **NINE MONTHS** TO DRAW, AND THE SECOND CHAPTER TOOK ME **A YEAR AND A HALF!**

AND IN THIS CHAPTER, IT'S **SNOWING,** WHICH TAKES EVEN **MORE** TIME TO DRAW...

10x

SIGH

IF YOU READ **PHASE 7** #010 AND #011, YOU KNOW HOW MUCH THIS STRESSES ME OUT!

BL BLA

I'M CONSTANTLY COMING UP WITH **NEW** STORIES THAT I WANT TO DRAW, ISSUES OF PHASE 7 I WANT TO FILL!

BUT I KNOW I'D NEVER BE ABLE TO LIVE WITH MYSELF IF I DIDN'T FINISH BASEWOOD.

AND I KNOW I WILL NEVER BE MORE PROUD OF ANYTHING I'VE EVER DONE, WHEN IT'S COMPLETE.

SO THE TRICK IS, FIGURING OUT HOW TO DO THAT, WITHOUT TAKING ANOTHER EIGHT YEARS....

ON AUGUST FIRST, 2004 I MOVED TO NEW YORK CITY.

I WANTED TO GO TO ART SCHOOL, BUT I WASN'T SURE IF I COULD DEAL WITH LIVING IN THE CITY.

I DEFERRED FOR ONE YEAR AND WORKED IN THE CITY BEFORE MAKING MY DECISION.

NEW YORK IS AN AMAZING PLACE, BUT IT IS ALSO A DIFFICULT PLACE TO LIVE

IT'S CROWDED

AND EXPENSIVE

SPARE SOME CHANGE MISTER?

AND ABOUT 3,000 MILES AWAY FROM THE REST OF MY FAMILY.

WA

SEATTLE

IN THE END, I DID DECIDE TO GO TO ART SCHOOL THOUGH. I DON'T REGRET IT.

THERE IS NO BETTER PLACE IN THE WORLD TO STUDY ART, THAN NEW YORK!

LOOK AT VAN GOGH'S TECHNIQUE HERE...

THE MET

IT WAS EXTREMELY HARD TO WORK ON BASEWOOD DURING ART SCHOOL, AND ALMOST **IMPOSSIBLE** TO DO SO AFTER IT WAS OVER!

GOTTA DO THIS PAYING WORK TO MAKE **RENT!**

IT WAS THEN THAT I REALIZED I HAD TO LEAVE NEW YORK.

BUT WHERE WILL I GO?

SEATTLE?

PORTLAND?

I NEED A PLACE WHERE IT'S CHEAPER TO LIVE, SO I WON'T HAVE TO WORK AS MUCH...

A PLACE WHERE IT'S QUIETER, WITH FEWER DISTRACTIONS...

WAIT! **I KNOW!**

the CENTER for CARTOON STUDIES

in WHITE RIVER JUNCTION, VERMONT!

I HAVE BEEN INVOLVED WITH THE SCHOOL SINCE IT BEGAN IN 2005, LECTURING ON SELF-PUBLISHING

AND HELPING OUT WITH THE SUMMER WORKSHOPS.

THE LAST TIME I WAS UP AT THE SCHOOL, I TALKED TO JAMES STURM (THE DIRECTOR)

HEY JAMES, I WAS THINKING OF APPLYING FOR THE FELLOWSHIP FOR NEXT YEAR.

I DON'T THINK THAT WOULD BE A PROBLEM.

SUDDENLY, I HAD **A PLAN!**

AT THE END OF JULY, 2008, I PACKED UP ALL OF MY STUFF

AND MOVED TO BEAUTIFUL VERMONT!

AFTER YEARS OF LIVING IN CLAUSTROPHOBIC NEW YORK APARTMENTS, I WAS FINALLY ABLE TO AFFORD A NICE PLACE... WITH **NO** ROOMMATES!

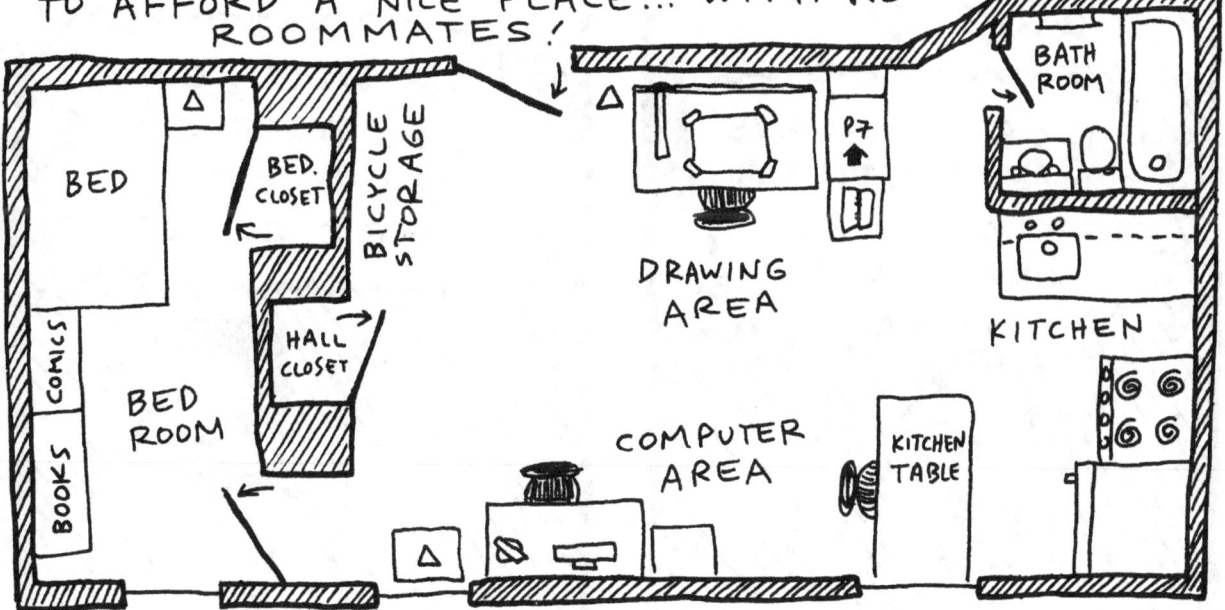

AND WHITE RIVER JUNCTION **DEFINITELY** FULFILLED MY REQUIREMENTS ABOUT BEING QUIETER, WITH FEWER DISTRACTIONS.

MAIN STREET (WHICH IS PRETTY MUCH THE **ONLY** STREET)

SOMETIMES IT CAN BE A LITTLE **TOO** QUIET...

I CAN'T BELIEVE THIS! **EVERYTHING** IS CLOSED BY NINE O'CLOCK!

BUT USUALLY THIS WORKS OUT WELL!

AH WELL, GUESS I'LL JUST GO DRAW SOME MORE COMICS!

WHEN I FIRST ARRIVED IN TOWN, I STILL HAD TO FINISH RE-LETTERING A BUNCH OF MY COMICS IN FRENCH, FOR AN UPCOMING **PHASE 7** COLLECTION FROM L'employé du moi.

IT WAS A LOT OF TEDIOUS WORK, BUT THE FRENCH BOOK WILL LOOK BETTER FOR IT, SO I DON'T MIND.

(COMING NOV. 2008!)

ONCE THAT WAS DONE, IT WAS TIME TO OFFICIALLY GET BACK TO WORK ON BASEWOOD!

AND SO, ON AUGUST FIRST, 2008 I CUT ALL OF MY HAIR (AND BEARD) OFF IN A RE-DEDICATION CEREMONY

MY GOAL IS TO NEVER CUT MY HAIR AGAIN UNTIL BASEWOOD IS COMPLETE.

I EXPECT THIS TO TAKE AT LEAST ANOTHER TWO YEARS (IF I WORK HARD)

EACH TIME I FINISH PENCILING OR INKING A PAGE OF BASEWOOD, I WILL POST A PICTURE OF MY BEARD IN MY FLICKR ACCOUNT:

http://www.flickr.com/photos/longstreth/

MY MOM **HATES** THAT I AM DOING THIS WITH MY HEAD.

HRMPH!

BUT I THINK IT WILL BE FUN. I'VE NEVER **REALLY** GROWN MY HAIR OR BEARD OUT BEFORE, AND IT SEEMS LIKE VERMONT IS A GOOD PLACE TO DO IT!

HULLO.

HI!

IT WILL KEEP ME WARM DURING THE LONG WINTER

AND HOPEFULLY THE VISUAL REMINDER WILL LEND ME SOME SUPPORT FROM MY FELLOW CARTOONISTS.

HOW'S BASEWOOD COMING ALONG?

SLOWLY, BUT SURELY!

PERHAPS I COULD EVEN CUT MY HAIR AT THE BOOK RELEASE PARTY!

FOR NOW, IT IS JUST A RELIEF TO HAVE SOME MONEY SAVED UP, A CLEAR SCHEDULE AND A GREAT PLACE TO DRAW!

IT HAS BEEN REALLY AWESOME TOO, HAVING ACCESS TO THE C.C.S. LIBRARY...

ALL COMICS!

ALSO, THE C.C.S. **LAB!**

BEEP!

SHORTLY AFTER MY ARRIVAL IN VERMONT, I RECEIVED TWO LARGE PHASE 7 ORDERS.

HMMM... I'LL HAVE TO PRINT OUT SOME NEW COPIES.

LAB COMPUTER

IT TURNS OUT, I CAN LOAD DIGITAL .PDFs INTO THE COPIER. SO I JUST HIT A BUTTON AND IT SPITS OUT A COPY OF PHASE 7!

THIS IS AMAZING!

WHIRRRRRRRR

IN NEW YORK, THIS WOULD HAVE INVOLVED TWO SUBWAY RIDES, LUGGING HEAVY BOXES, HAGGLING WITH THE PRINTER, AND CONSTANTLY TRYING TO GUESS THE RIGHT QUANTITY TO BUY.

IS 100 ENOUGH? CAN I AFFORD 200?

NOW IT'S LIKE I HAVE A PHASE 7 PRINT-ON-DEMAND MACHINE!

THANKS PHOTOCOPIER!

NO SWEAT ALEC!

BESIDES ALL OF THE FANCY EQUIPMENT, I AM ALSO **EXTREMELY** EXCITED TO HANG OUT ALL YEAR WITH THE IMMENSELY TALENTED INSTRUCTORS AND STAFF MEMBERS OF C.C.S.

JAMES STURM

SATCHEL PAIGE, THE GOLEM'S MIGHTY SWING, J.S.'S AMERICA

JASON LUTES

JAR OF FOOLS, BERLIN, THE FALL

STEVE BISSETTE

TYRANT, SWAMP THING, TABOO

CHRIS WRIGHT

INKWEED, MY FELLOW FELLOW!

ROBYN CHAPMAN

SOUR PUSS, HEY 4-EYES!, TRUE PORN

JON CHAD

LEO GEO, WHALETOWNE

I KNOW I'M GOING TO LEARN A LOT THIS YEAR!

AND NOT JUST FROM THE FACULTY! I'M PUMPED TO HANG OUT AND LEARN FROM ALL THE C.C.S. ALUMNI WHO STILL LIVE IN TOWN, AND THE CURRENT SECOND-YEARS, WITH WHOM I WILL BE SHARING STUDIO SPACE!

AND ON TOP OF ALL THAT, I ALSO GET TO MEET THE 24 NEW, INCOMING FIRST-YEARS! WHO KNOWS WHAT NEW FRIENDS HIDE IN THEIR RANKS? I CAN'T WAIT TO FIND OUT!

HOPEFULLY, THIS WILL MEAN A NEW ISSUE OF PHASE 7 WINGING ITS WAY TO SUBSCRIBERS IN EARLY 2009.

#007

48 PAGES

IF YOU ARE A SUBSCRIBER, I APPRECIATE YOUR CONTINUED PATIENCE.

THANKS TO ALL THE FRIENDS I MADE IN NEW YORK CITY...

AND THANKS IN ADVANCE TO ALL MY NEW FRIENDS IN VERMONT!

♡ALE. WHITE RIVER JUNCTION, VT-9/2/2008

MY FELLOWSHIP YEAR AT C.C.S. WAS **AMAZING!** AFTER IT WAS OVER, I DECIDED TO STAY IN WHITE RIVER JUNCTION.

AND AS YOU CAN SEE, I AM STILL HARD AT WORK ON **BASEWOOD.**

THE FELLOW FOR THE YEAR AFTER ME WAS **MAX DE RADIGUÈS** FROM BRUSSELS, BELGIUM!

MAX WORKS AT L'EMPLOYÉ DU MOI AND IS ONE OF THE GUYS WHO TRANSLATED MY FRENCH PHASE 7 BOOK.

DURING A LONG TRAIN RIDE TO NEW YORK CITY, MAX AND I DREW A COLLABORATIVE COMIC IN OUR SKETCHBOOKS.

HA HA HA HA HA

HA

IT WAS SO MUCH FUN, WE DECIDED TO DO A 24-HOUR COMIC TOGETHER! BEFORE WE STARTED THOUGH, WE WATCHED "NOTHING SACRED" AND "COVER GIRL" FOR INSPIRATION.

WE ALSO CHECKED OUT SOME PHOTOGRAPHY BOOKS FROM THE C.C.S. LIBRARY, FOR REFERENCE (AS YOU'LL SEE).

"NAKED CITY" BY WEEGEE

"THE PAM ARTIST" WAS DRAWN ON DECEMBER 5TH, 2009 FROM 12AM TO 10:41 PM. I HOPE YOU LIKE IT!

the
PAM
artist

A 24-HOUR COMIC DRAWN ON 12/5/09 BY MAX DE RADIGUÈS & ALÉ LONGSTRETH

NEW YORK PENN STATION IN TEN MINUTES

TICKE

TIMES BY BENERUS

INCOMING TRAINS

145

146

155

SHOULD I FOLLOW?

OR MAYBE...

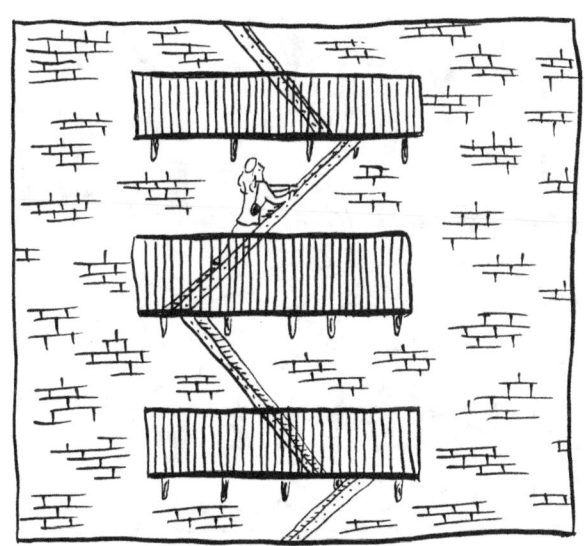

www.ingramcontent.com/pod-product-compliance
Lightning Source LLC
Chambersburg PA
CBHW080734250626
47170CB00010B/2827